Scrapbooks of America™

Published by Tradition Books® and distributed to the school and library market by The Child's World®
P.O. Box 326, Chanhassen, MN 55317-0326 ➝ 800/599-READ ➝ http://www.childsworld.com

Photo Credits: Cover: Michael Maslan Historic Photographs/Corbis; Bettmann/Corbis: 13, 17, 24, 28, 30, 35; Corbis: 7, 12, 25, 31, 34, 40; Richard Cummins/Corbis: 18; Leonard deSelva/Corbis: 10; Roger Garwood & Trish Ainslie/Corbis: 21; Rob Howard/Corbis: 22(right); Michael Maslan Historic Photographs/Corbis: 16, 39; Museum of History & Industry/Corbis: 11, 15, 22(left); Royalty-Free/Corbis: 6, 38; Paul A. Souders/Corbis: 9

An Editorial Directions book
Editorial Directions, Inc.: E. Russell Primm, Editorial Director; Lucia Raatma, Line Editor, Photo Selector, and Additional Writing; Katie Marsico, Assistant Editor; Olivia Nellums, Editorial Assistant; Susan Hindman, Copy Editor; Susan Ashley, Proofreader; Alice Flanagan, Photo Researcher and Additional Writer

Design: The Design Lab

Library of Congress Cataloging-in-Publication Data
Cataloging-in-Publication data for this title has been applied for and is available from the United States Library of Congress.

Scrapbooks of America™

HALF-BREED

A Story of the Klondike Gold Rush

by Pamela Dell

TRADITION BOOKS®
A New Tradition in Children's Publishing™
MAPLE PLAIN, MINNESOTA

Table of Contents

Ike's Story, page 6

"Come gee!" I commanded, in a calm, firm voice. "Come gee!"

The February wind was cruel, its **harsh** fingertips needling against my face as we sped along. With feet planted firmly on the sled's runners, I let go with one hand and wiped an arm across my eyes, hoping to brush some of the tiny ice crystals from my lashes. We were racing into a white swirl of snow, and I could see no farther than a few yards ahead even now. Before long, it would be dark. But I had heard something. We had to go back.

"Come gee!" Without even slowing from her hard speed, Pika immediately obeyed my command. Her woolly silver head and power-

Pika was a special dog, and I knew I could always count on her.

The 1890s marked a difficult time in the United States. Businesses were failing, and banks were closing. Many people lost their jobs. So some left for Alaska, with the hope of finding gold—and getting rich.

Alaska could be a rough place if you were lost or alone in the wilderness.

ful shoulders leaned into a right turn, and she began to circle back, carving a perfect 180-degree arc in the snow. The eight other team dogs ran as a single unit behind her, keeping the turn going and our speed constant.

I kept my eyes trained on Pika, confident of her ability to know my mind and to find what we were looking for. Her ears were pricked forward, assuring me she had heard the cry of distress, just as I had. Somewhere in the white wilderness behind us, someone was calling for help.

The cry came again, closer. This time without even a word from me, Pika altered our course slightly in the direction of the sound.

"Easy," I commanded, as we came out of a clearing and into a more densely wooded area. The dogs slowed at once. In my mind a single thought echoed repeatedly: *Find him, Pika.* These words in my head were like a beam of light traveling up to her in front. It had always been like that, even since she had been just a small bundle of Alaskan Husky fur a few weeks old. We communicated with perfect understanding and often with no words at all. She had an instinct for knowing things beyond what her five senses picked up. She was true, and she was brave. She worked hard and enjoyed it, had always shown a natural willingness to be a leader with the other dogs. That was why she was my lead dog—and my best companion.

Now Pika yelped slightly and bounded forward. In a moment, despite the snow blowing so fiercely around us, a gray outline came into view a few yards ahead. It looked like a large round stone or a lumpy potato sack.

We pulled up, and I put heavy pressure on the brake, commanding the dogs to stop at the same time.

"Whoa!" Pika and the others came to a halt, breathing hard, and the **towline** went slack. I jumped off and drove the **snow hook** into the crusty whiteness to keep the dogs in place. Then I approached the moaning lump of potato sack where it sat beneath a towering spruce tree. Nearby but flung to the side were a pair of **snowshoes,** one of them badly damaged.

Dog sled teams were common in Alaska and were especially needed during the gold rush.

As I came to stand above it, the lump looked up at me. Its blue eyes were bright with fear, its plump cheeks chapped red as bear's blood. It was a white boy about thirteen, my own age. Just looking at him, I knew his story. He was a gold rush kid, part of some family that had rushed up from the United States to this Alaskan territory in a fever for getting rich. Just like all the thousands of others who had been arriving since the summer before for the same thing.

"Help," he said weakly. I did not reply but squatted as he reached down and put two mittened hands protectively around his ankle. I pushed his hands away and placed my own bare fingers against the bone where he had loosened his boot.

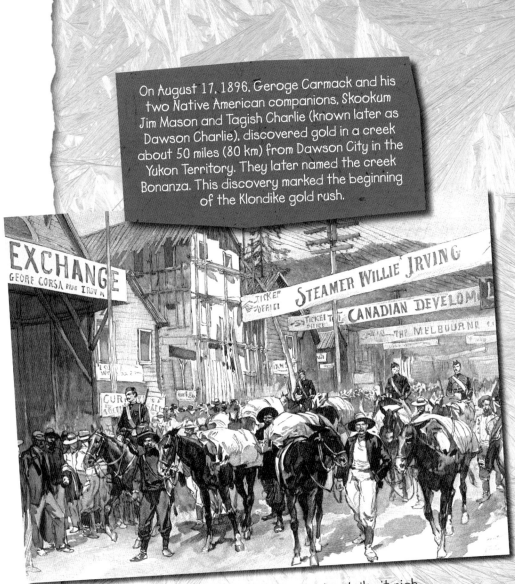

On August 17, 1896, Geroge Carmack and his two Native American companions, Skookum Jim Mason and Tagish Charlie (known later as Dawson Charlie), discovered gold in a creek about 50 miles (80 km) from Dawson City in the Yukon Territory. They later named the creek Bonanza. This discovery marked the beginning of the Klondike gold rush.

People flocked to Alaska, hoping to strike it rich, and gold mining towns became busy places.

The Chilkoot Pass led from the town of Dyea to Lake Lindeman, in Canada, and was 32 miles (51 km) long. Before the gold rush, the Tlingit Indians had used the trail for hundreds of years.

Traveling the Chilkoot Pass was a dangerous undertaking, no matter what equipment you had.

"It's broke, I think," he said. "I was hiking and fell off a ledge. I didn't see it, on account of the snow. I broke it bad."

I shook my head. His ankle bones were all where they were meant to be, but the flesh was swollen. It was only a sprain.

"It is broke!" His voice sounded both **insistent** and helpless, even silly to my ears. I knew of boys his age who had made it over one of the steepest, most dangerous trails anywhere in Alaska—the Chilkoot Pass. The last terrible half-mile of that trail, known as the Golden Staircase, took a body up 1,500 steps carved in the ice, with nothing but a thin guide rope to hang onto.

Ever since the summer before, hundreds of hope-driven men, boys, and even women had been heading out from the little town of Dyea. All of them were bent on making it over that pass and on to the Klondike gold fields. Stampeders, we called them.

I'd been up part of that route myself many times, carrying their loads for pay. Sometimes, if they offered me enough, I'd even haul baggage as far as Sheep Camp, the last real settlement before that sheer, **wicked** climb to the top. I got paid plenty for making that trip. Other days I made my money in a lot easier ways than that. With men everywhere mad for gold, it was easy to make money.

Men mad for gold saw visions of huge fortunes dug from the frozen ground. Those visions got them up the trails carrying loads

Prospectors at Sheep Camp, the last place to rest before tackling Chilkoot Pass

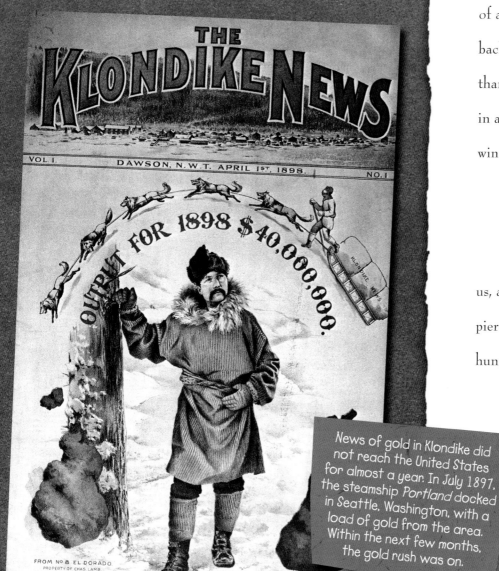

News of gold in Klondike did not reach the United States for almost a year. In July 1897, the steamship *Portland* docked in Seattle, Washington, with a load of gold from the area. Within the next few months, the gold rush was on.

The cover of *The Klondike News* on April 1, 1898

of a hundred pounds or more on their backs—and sometimes with injuries worse than the one this sack of potatoes slumped in a snowdrift had. So he was not about to win my pity.

"Get up," I said.

"I can't!"

The wind was whistling hard between us, and off in the distance I heard a long, piercing howl. A wolf. Probably a lone and hungry one, too.

"What was that?" the boy asked, looking around.

I put my hands on my hips and gazed down at him. I couldn't help smiling. "A wolf," I told him calmly. "Looking for his dinner."

Instantly the boy began to struggle, trying to get to his feet, trying to move his bulky body into a standing position. But he was bundled in so much fur and **canvas** that he could barely move. I reached down, grabbed fast to his upper arm, and pulled him up. He stood on his right leg, his other bent at the knee and his foot not quite touching the ground. Standing, he was almost exactly my own height. Our eyes met up close.

"Get in my sled," I said, nodding in that direction. "I'll take you back to Skagway."

"How do you know that's where I'm going?" the boy asked in a wary voice.

It hadn't taken much sense to figure it out. I'd been only a couple of miles out of Skagway and heading home to Dyea when I'd heard his cries. There was no way he had hiked all the way from Dyea, ten miles north of Skagway, to this spot. Just no way.

Skagway was the other jumping-off point for stampeders traveling on foot. They were all aiming for the boomtown of Dawson City in Canada. From there, the Klondike River gold fields—and all those riches they dreamed of—were just a step away. But it was 1898, and the feverish prospecting up there had been going on for nearly two years already. Even if the stampeders survived the climb up the trail and down the other side, it was still winter. There would be no way to get to Dawson until the lakes and rivers thawed come spring. But by then they'd be lucky if they even found an empty spot to stake a claim.

Dawson City was a bustling town, quite close to the Klondike gold fields.

Chilkoot was the more popular route over the **summit,** but a lot of people left from Skagway, taking White Pass over. It was a longer route, but it was wide and easy starting out. They figured they could haul wagons and sleds up that way. What they didn't know, or maybe didn't take seriously, was that the pass turned into something else all too soon. A few miles up, White Pass became a terror trail, only two feet wide in some spots. Horses, sled dogs, and even men had been known to lose their footing and **pitch** hundreds of feet straight down to their deaths. And frequently, too. Some even called it Dead Horse Trail for all the bodies of broken animals lying in the **muck** and snow along the way.

White Pass Trail had some terrible spots, places where dogs and horses could easily stumble and fall.

These miners—and thousands of others—took a big chance by coming to Alaska during the gold rush.

Looking at this boy, I knew he wouldn't be going up either one of those passes, even if he had two healthy legs. But most likely his daddy was suffering up there somewhere in the name of riches, even now.

"Come on," I said. We were standing in a thick gray fog of swirling snow. Even the outlines of the trees were barely visible. "Got to move quick."

"You tell me your name before I go anywhere on that thing," the boy demanded. "And what your business is, too." As far as I was concerned, he didn't need to know a thing about me, but I decided to satisfy him halfway.

"They call me Ike FitzHugh," I said. The boy's eyes narrowed at once.

THE WHITE PASS CHRONICLE

GROWING WITH THE LAST GREAT FRONTIER

NEWS FROM THE KLONDIKE

GOLD! GOLD! GOLD! GOLD!

Special Tug Chartered To Get The New

The Land Of Gold

...gons Running

...dream dreams.
...ay sheer walls
...2, 1898, it ran
...sion of man's
...timeless march

...onomic depres-
...ntific advance-

...haps within the
...bile will zoom
...eds. Man may
...take to the air
...of nations will
...who are still to
...common cold.
...ay sound, frail
...d his footprints

WHITE HORSE TODAY

BUILDING BOOMING

White Horse, Apr. 1, 1901 — The spring boom has struck White Horse in earnest. The sound of hammers can be heard in all directions and vacant lots in the business portion of the town are becoming as scarce as mushrooms on an iceberg.

Many substantial frame buildings are going up, also many canvas ones which in time will give place to more permanent structures.

About 400 men are at present working in the town with the prospect of many more being employed, and in the evening the streets put one in mind of the great thoroughfares of the large cities throughout the states.

SKAGWAY AND UP RIVER POINTS

Alex Schwartz and Party
Leave Bennett By Boat

Seattle, July 17, 1897. ON BOARD THE STEAMSHIP POR[T]LAND, 3:00 A.M. — At 3 o'clock this morning the steams[hip] Portland, from St. Michaels for Seattle, passed up [the] Sound with more than a ton of solid gold on board and [68] passengers. In the captain's cabin are three chests and [a] large safe filled with the precious nuggets. The metal [is] worth nearly $700,000 and most of it was taken from [the] Klondike district in less than three months last winter. [In] size the nuggets range from the size of a pea to a guin[ea] hen egg. Of the 68 miners on board hardly a man has l[ess] than $7,000, and one or two have more than $100,000 [in] yellow nuggets.

Clarence Berry is regarded as the luc[kiest] man in the Klondike. Ten months ago he [was] a poor miner and to-day he is in S[eattle] with $130,000 in gold nuggets. One n[ugget] weighs 13 ounces and is worth $231. [He has] been rather fortunate," he averred.

Inspector Strickland, of the North [West] Mounted Police, was guarded with [his] statements. He said there were only [two] mining districts in what is known a[s the] Klondike section and they are called [the] Hunker and Bonanza districts. He a[dded,] "When I left Dawson City, a mont[h ago]

QUEEN VICTORIA

Newspapers fed the excitement people felt about the gold rush,
luring prospectors to the Klondike.

"You a **half-breed?**" he blurted.

The moment those words of his hit the air, I turned abruptly and began making my way back to the sled.

"Hey!" he snapped, talking to my back. "I asked you something! You just walk off?"

"Stay here and be a wolf's dinner, fine with me," I replied. I had to shout it because I was moving fast and the storm was blowing hard. I didn't even look back as I let my words fly. I came up to my dogs and gave each one a long stroke, knelt down and wrapped my arm tight around Pika's neck. She responded with a happy slap against my cheek with her wet tongue. The weather didn't look like it was going to get any better, but I knew she'd get us back. Just had to move it before dark though.

Pika was a half-breed, too—so what? Half-wolf, half-Siberian, or some such mixed-up mix, that was the thing with Alaskan Huskies. But what of it? She was finer, more intelligent and loyal, than any pure breed a person could think of. I already knew that people who made a big fuss over pure breeds didn't have a clue about what counted most: how you made your way in the world, not who or what you came from.

I busied myself feeding my dogs a few pounds of salmon and making sure all the sled rigging was tight. I had a full load that I'd picked up from a stampeder in Skagway who wanted his stuff transported to Dyea.

So if anybody was going to ride with me I had some rearranging to do.

It wasn't too long before the potato sack came dragging himself through the drifting snow, trying to use his snowshoes as short crutches. He half-hopped, half-limped right up to where we stood, getting ready to take off again.

His eyes met mine once more, and we stared hard at one another, a struggle between my black-sky eyes and his blue ice. Sky won, and he looked off at the dogs.

"What's her name?" he asked, meaning Pika. He wobbled slightly on one foot.

I strapped down the food tin and tightened the harnesses on both wheel dogs, the two positioned directly in front of the sled.

"Kappiataitok Pikatti," I said finally.

"What?" The boy's nose wrinkled up like he had a problem of some sort. I straightened and looked right at him, then spoke every syllable so clear anybody could understand.

"Kappia. Tai. Tok. 'Brave,' in English. Pikatti. 'Companion.' Or maybe 'partner.'"

"'Brave partner,' huh?" he repeated. "Let's hope so." He didn't even try to repeat the **Inuit** words I had just spoken to him. Words that came from my mother's language. There was no doubt in my mind he didn't even know the word Inuit. As far as I'd seen, most whites bunched every different native people into one general group and just called it Eskimo, simple and mindless as that. My own father was the only white man I knew

When some lucky people did find gold, they knew they were holding small fortunes in their hands.

The gold rush changed everything for native Indians in the Yukon Territory. Before 1896, three of every four people in the region were Indian. By 1901, there was only one Indian for every eight non-native people.

An Inuit couple dressed for the harsh weather of Alaska

For many of us, having dogs was an important part of our lives.

who was intelligent enough to make the **distinctions** among the Tlingit, the Athabascan and the Inupiaq peoples.

"I just call her Pika," I offered. "Get in, we're going."

"But my pack!" the boy said, gesturing back toward the trees. I turned and saw a heavy-looking bag in the snow where he'd been sitting.

"Can't take it," I said. "Too full."

"But it's my stuff!"

I gave it only a second's thought. "I'll pick it up on my way back to Dyea," I said. "Then I'll bring it to you in Skagway tomorrow when I come in again."

I could see he didn't like that idea one bit but he had no choice. It was either him or the bag. I took a length of rope, tied the pack to it, looped the other end over a high tree branch, and strung it up tight so it wouldn't fall. It dangled in the air but it was secure.

"So no critters get at it," I explained, coming back to the sled and helping him get settled there.

"Mush!" the boy cried, as soon as he'd sat down and I'd stepped on the runners. Pika and the others looked back at him, but none of them even twitched.

"Just so you know," I said, with a little bristle in my voice, "my dogs won't listen to you—you, whatever your name is."

"It's Stuart Clapp," the boy replied, like it meant something important. "From Seattle."

"Hike!" I commanded. As we started to pull off, I made a loud kissing sound to let my dogs know I didn't want to just get going—I wanted to go fast. *Mush* was a word I never used to get a dog sled moving. It was just too soft, like the potato sack named Stuart.

The main street of Skagway was as overactive as usual. Unlike Dyea, where people unloaded from the boats right onto the beach itself, Skagway had docking facilities and a deeper harbor. Some of the ships, once they got up to Skagway, just didn't bother going on to Dyea at all, even if their passengers had paid to get there. That meant anyone bent on taking the Chilkoot Pass needed to get them-

During the gold rush, Skagway grew into a town that was home to thousands of people.

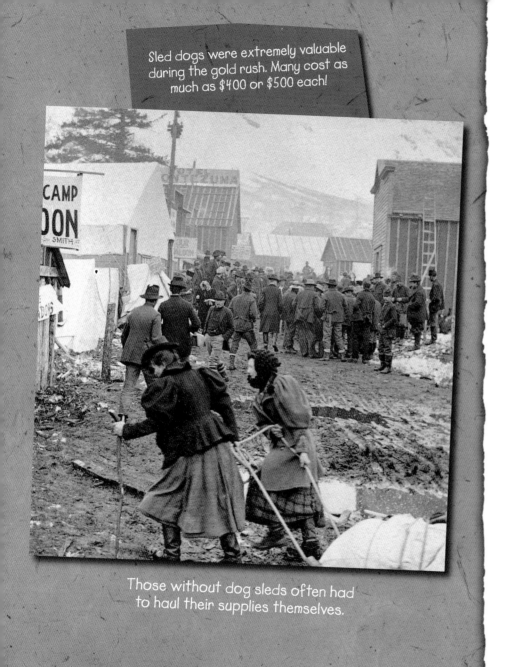

Sled dogs were extremely valuable during the gold rush. Many cost as much as $400 or $500 each!

Those without dog sleds often had to haul their supplies themselves.

selves and their belongings the rest of the way. That was another way I made easy money.

I needed as much money as I could get, too. I needed cash to keep my sled and all the **rigging** in good shape. Cash to add new treasures to my collection of hunting knives. And most of all, I was planning to build my dogs the finest kennel anywhere around as soon as it began to thaw. That would take a bundle, I knew. So Skagway was my own little gold mine.

The snowstorm was dying down, but there were few daylight hours left and I wanted to get home as soon as I could. I had half a mind to set Stu on a corner and let him limp his way to wherever he was going from there. All the way into town he had

pestered me with questions about my dogs and about sledding. That was in between giving me all the details on his particular story, of course, though I hadn't asked for any.

As it turned out, Stu already had an aunt and two uncles in Alaska. The three of them had come up the fall before, right after hearing about the Klondike gold rush. They'd started up White Pass, but only the older of the two uncles had kept on. After a few horrifying days on the pass, uncle number two and his wife had given up and turned back. For now they were making their home in Skagway and, according to Stu, bringing up Chinooks to sell as sled dogs.

Now Stu's father meant to get to Dawson and catch up with his brother there. Rather than leaving them alone in Seattle, he'd dragged Stu and his mother up to Skagway to stay with the aunt and uncle until he returned.

Alaskan Huskies are sometimes called Eskimo dogs.

Hearing this, and the tone of his voice as he told me, I realized Stu had probably been out hiking with all that gear on his back just to prove he had what it took to make it to Dawson. No doubt hoping his father would take him along. But there was sure no hope in that now.

There was a long silence between us after he had filled me in on all that. Then as we were pulling into Skagway, his voice brightened.

"My old man's going to come back richer

than a king!" Stu exclaimed. I wanted to laugh right out loud, but I just slowed the sled and pulled over on the main street into town.

"Where's your aunt's?" I asked. I was hoping to dump Stu there as quickly as I could and get on home. But he immediately started struggling to get up and off the sled.

"You were right," he said. "My ankle's not broke. I'll make it from here."

"Shouldn't walk on that," I advised. "Stay put."

But Stu was stubborn. He hobbled off a few steps as I watched, saying nothing. But I could see he wasn't going to get far on his own. I tied the dogs down and came to his side, hooking his arm around my shoulders. That didn't please him at all and he pushed me away. In a minute, though, he wised up and gave in.

"Just take me as far as that hotel right up there," Stu said as we limped along. "They know my relatives." I noticed his eyes were roaming the streets, nervously, like he was on the lookout for something. And then there it was. A man came barreling out of a **saloon** and blocked our path. Stuart froze.

"Dad!" he said. His face went pale, and right away his arm came off my shoulder. He **teetered** as he tried to stand on his own.

The man looked at Stu, then at me, and back to his son, an expression of plain

In May 1898, Dyea boasted forty-eight hotels, forty-seven restaurants, and thirty-nine saloons. Somewhere between 5,000 and 8,000 people lived there.

These men in Dawson City weighed their gold and used it as payment in a local store.

disgust growing on his face. "What kind of nonsense you pulling here, Stuart?" he said, in a voice colder than the day.

"Nothing, Dad," Stu said meekly. "I just bruised my ankle is all."

"Boy, you letting some Eskimo carry you down the street in full view of the whole town? Who's son are you? Get home, you hear me? And get there on your own two feet!"

Mr. Clapp turned to me.

"And you," he said. "Get away from my son. I don't want to see you anywhere around here, you understand, Eskimo?"

I stood my ground for a moment without a word, while Stu moved past his father and kept going. It wasn't pretty watching him trying to walk without limping. Then I turned my back on both of them and was gone.

❧

By the time I reached Dyea, dark was biting down hard on the land and the northern lights were doing their awesome dance of color in the night sky. I'd had to stop and bring Stu's pack down from the tree, of course, but Pika had had no trouble finding it at all.

Next day, I was back in Skagway early, planning to hire out to the first stampeder in need of a sled. But first I had to deliver a dozen loaves of bread my mother had baked for a couple of Skagway's restaurants, take orders for more, and then see about getting Stu's pack back to him. My mother's fresh bread was in big demand in both Skagway and Dyea, so she was able to sell each loaf for a whopping $40. That was a dollar less than some charged, and it was better tasting than theirs, too.

After my deliveries, I left the backpack at the hotel Stu had pointed out the day before. The manager there knew the Clapp family well and assured me Stu would get his belongings back immediately, a thing I was glad to hear. I was done with Stu myself, and I didn't at all welcome another run-in with his father either.

The minute I was free of all that, I parked my dogs down by the Taiya River. I planned to spend an hour before the ship came in the way I often did, inspecting the

By June 1898, with an estimated population of 8,800 to 10,000 people, Skagway was the largest city in Alaska.

Stores like this one in Skagway sold all kinds of merchandise that the miners needed.

A ship arriving in Skagway. Miners often arrived
at this harbor before heading to the gold fields.

hunting and trapping gear at the various shops in town. If I saw something I liked, I'd cut a good deal or make a trade of some sort. Then I'd go back down to the harbor and find myself that transporting job.

But it didn't turn out quite like that.

As I approached the harbor, I could hear the howl of dogs. There were a lot of loose dogs in town, poor **mangy** mutts that had been abandoned the spring before, once they were no longer useful. After months on their own, they were often vicious and carrying **rabies.** I stepped up my pace, thinking my team might be in trouble.

As I came to the place I'd **staked** them down, I saw there was trouble, all right, but it wasn't the kind I was expecting at all. My eight team dogs were just where I'd left them, moving restlessly, yelping and pushing, as if they were mightily upset about something. I knew instantly what it was too. Pika's harness was lying empty in the snow, and she was plain gone.

I got to the sled running and tried to settle my dogs while calling for Pika at the same time. I howled out her name at the top of my lungs. I whistled loud enough to pierce an eardrum, expecting to see her come galloping in my direction from around some corner. But that didn't happen. All I saw were the eyes on me, the eyes of people who weren't happy to see a crazed boy making a big fuss down at the docks. As they passed, a few of those white people who thought themselves so well-bred and civilized swore at me. Others told me to keep quiet as they passed wide around me. I heard the names they used against me, every one. Names that made my teeth grind and my jaw go tight. Names that reminded me of Stu and his remark the day before when I'd told him my name.

But I was frantic and didn't care how much noise I made. I had to find my dog. All at once somebody grabbed me roughly from behind. I jerked away and turned to find Stu glaring at me. He was leaning on crutches now, and the hard look on his face made me think right away of his father.

"Your dog's gone, half-breed," he said. I took a deep breath, working to stay calm. When I didn't say anything, Stu spoke again.

"You're not getting her back either."

"Where is she?" If the sound of those words leaving my mouth could have a shape, I thought, it would look like a thin and dangerously jagged line.

"She's gone," Stu repeated. "Just like my *stuff* is gone."

"What stuff?"

"My stuff you stole," he said simply.

I waited, staring at him.

"The little bag that was hanging off my pack. With the knife and the money in it," he added.

"Give me my dog back, Stu," I said finally, in a low, even voice, "or you'll never see your stuff."

"I knew it," Stu sneered. "You're all just

what my dad said you were."

"Give me my dog."

Stu shrugged and turned his head. He looked off toward the water as if the dockside activity was the most interesting thing in the world and I didn't even exist. Watching him like that brought a sudden unexpected fire to my body. My hands came out, and I snatched both crutches right from under him. He wasn't prepared for it either and he lost his balance, toppling to the ground as I watched. I loomed over him, holding the crutches behind my back.

"You show me where my dog is, and you'll get your bag back. That's it." I could feel my eyes spitting fire down on him—and he, I could tell, felt it, too.

Traveling in the Klondike region got easier when the White Pass and Yukon Railroad was built. Construction began in May 1898. By the time it was finished, the project cost more than $10 million.

Many of the gold miners camped in tents like these during their journey into the Yukon.

Dogs were not the only animals in demand during the gold rush. Some stampeders also bought horses and goats. Horses could carry packs and pull wagons. Goats provided milk and were sure-footed on steep hills.

Prospectors needed lots of equipment, but getting it all to the gold fields was a challenge.

"All right," he said, holding a hand up over his face as if I might attack him. It would have been easy to hurt him, maybe kick him, or pound him in the gut with one of his own crutches. Some might have believed he even deserved such treatment, too. But that was the kind of behavior favored by powerless, fear-struck animals. Or the kind of thing greed-fevered gold hounds did to one another. It wasn't my way though. So instead, I stayed in my true power. I reached down and, for the second time in two days, helped Stu get to his feet. In my mind, I held the picture of him doing the right thing.

"Get in," I said. Stu looked fearfully at me.

"I'm not going to hurt you," I assured him. "We're going to get your stuff."

After I'd pushed him down, Stu had lain there terrified and nearly helpless. But once he'd realized I really wasn't going to harm him, he had let me help him up. Then, without too much more talk, he had led me to Pika. He'd tied her up in a dim alleyway, behind some half-broken-down old shack, and when she saw me she began yelping madly. Her tail switched back and forth in a frenzy of excitement as I untied her and hugged her to me. A few minutes later, we were all back at the sled and she was again harnessed in the lead.

Now it was time to move it. "Get in," I said again. This time Stu came forward and clumsily settled in the sled. After stowing the crutches securely beside him, I walked up to Pika at the head of the team. I squatted down and put my face into her fur, concentrating all my thought on what I wanted from her. I took the mitten of Stu's that I was holding and let her sniff it good. She was no mere **bloodhound;** she was something better. She was Kappiataitok Pikatti, half-breed.

I whispered in Pika's ear what we were going to do. Like I had with Stu, I focused my attention on exactly what I wanted. I pictured her understanding everything I needed her to know. Then I went back, jumped on the runners, and gave the command. In a few minutes, we were speeding out of Skagway, following our usual route back to Dyea.

This time Stu sat silently, his arms folded across his chest and his eyes straight ahead. I guided the dogs the first few miles, but when we neared the spot where I'd first found Stu injured, I called up to Pika.

"Okay, girl!" I said. "This is it. You know where to go." Then I relaxed into the ride and let my trust take over. As always when Pika and I began to focus intently together on the same thing, I felt a strange flow begin in my mind. It was almost like the **ebb** of the sea, the wash of the tide. Like a **current** that moved from deep within me to her, then back to me again. I couldn't even talk about that feeling, not to anyone, because it had no words, either in English or Inuit. It

was just the experience of being in **harmony.** Being in communication with another creature, a pure, effortless connection.

Abruptly, Pika headed the team off to the left, the two swing dogs just behind her continuing the curve and the wheel dogs moving out wide to keep us from whacking into a large boulder. Then she slowed and finally came to a stop without a word from me. She whined loudly and turned her face back to me. Her mouth was open and her tongue hung out as she panted hard. Looking at her, I was sure she was smiling.

It didn't take me long to find it. It was nearly hidden by a low bush and partly buried in snow, but there it was. A new-looking

The search for gold drew attention to Alaska. From 1890 to 1900, the region's population almost doubled, reaching more than 63,000.

deerskin bag with its drawstring pulled tight. I pulled the bag out, brushed it off, and opened it. I saw Stu limping his way toward me as I pulled out a good-sized knife held in a leather **sheath** with fancy stitching. The bag was heavy with coins, too.

I turned to Stu as he came toward me. "This yours?" I said.

The glimmer of respect in his face told me he understood what had happened, and the thought came to me that there was a chance he and I might even end up friends.

Of course the bag was his. But I hadn't stolen it. What goes around comes around. I didn't want that kind of action coming back on me, so stealing was one of many things I never even considered doing in my

Gold was found in other parts of Alaska, too. In 1898, gold was discovered in Nome, and four years later, it was discovered in Fairbanks.

His pouch didn't contain gold like this one, but Stuart sure was eager to find it.

During the 1800s, dog sleds were made of strong wood, usually birch, ash, or hickory. They could be anywhere from 6 to 14 feet (1.8 to 4.3 meters) long.

I often believed that my sled dogs were the truest friends I could ever hope for.

life. As I said, who you are is best measured by how you make your way in the world, not by what kind of blood your heart pumps out. The simple truth was that Stu's deerskin bag had accidentally fallen off his pack somewhere between Dyea and Skagway.

The other part of the truth was that the mind flow between Pika and me was like a kind of magic. That flow was invisible, sure, but it was everywhere, available to anybody. And it could accomplish amazing things if you knew how to use it. All Pika and I had done was trust it to lead us to where we needed to be. Under those conditions, that bag, and all its contents, had to be found. That's just the way it works.

The History of the Klondike Gold Rush

The Klondike is an area in the west central Yukon Territory of northwest Canada, close to the Alaskan border. Between 1896 and 1897, it was the site of a large-scale gold-mining activity known as the Klondike Gold Rush. On August 17, 1896, George W. Carmack and two Indian friends, Skookum Jim and Tagish Charlie, discovered gold on

Bonanza Creek. The creek, which flowed into the Klondike River, was near the present town of Dawson. Following the discovery, thousands of prospectors poured into the Yukon. By 1900, $22 million in gold had been mined by hand.

Native people, such as the Chilkoot and Chilkat bands of the Tlingit tribe, were important to the success of the Gold Rush. They, like Ike FitzHugh's Inuit ancestors, helped non-natives survive the harsh climate. For centuries, coastal tribes had traveled through the mountain passes to the interior on trading expeditions. The knowledge they acquired gave them control over the region and placed them in high demand after prospectors began arriving there.

The newcomers relied on native guides to take them over the mountains and carry their supplies. They bought the mukluks (boots made from animals skins) and other essential clothing native women made. And few miners would have survived without the meat and fish that native hunters and fishers supplied. Salmon was particularly important as dog food, especially in winter when dog teams were vital for transportation.

At the height of the Klondike Gold Rush, some 35,000 people lived in the Yukon Territory. Before 1896, Native Americans outnumbered non-natives by about 4 to 1. After the Gold Rush, non-natives outnumbered Native Americans by about 8 to 1. This sharp reversal of population within just two years created many problems for native people. They were often singled out and treated unfairly by non-natives. When would-be miners couldn't find gold and were desperate to make a living, they displaced native workers. Even today, when mining is still the most important industry of the Klondike region, Native Americans are struggling to achieve what they lost.

Glossary

bloodhound a breed of dog with a sharp sense of smell

canvas a woven, heavy cloth

current an electric charge or flow

distinctions qualities of being different

ebb the flowing back, like the movement of a sea's tide

half-breed someone with one Indian parent and one Caucasian parent

harmony a condition of everything being agreeable and pleasant

harsh unpleasant or cruel

insistent demanding and firm

Inuit the language of the Inuit, a group of Eskimos living in Greenland and throughout northwest Alaska

mangy shabby, or having a skin disease called the mange

muck dark, thick mud

pestered bothered or annoyed

pitch to plunge or fall forward

Timeline

1784 Russians begin the first white settlement in Alaska, located on Kodiak Island.

1848 Gold is discovered at Sutter's Mill in California, and a gold rush is underway by the next year.

1867 The United States buys Alaska from Russia.

1880 Joseph Juneau and Richard T. Harris find gold deposits in southeastern Alaska, leading to the creation of the city of Juneau.

1896 Rich gold deposits are discovered in the Klondike area of Canada's Yukon region, just over the border from Alaska.

1897 The Klondike gold rush begins and continues through 1898.

rabies a fatal disease of dogs, cats, and other animals, spread to humans by biting

rigging a system of ropes that control a dogsled

saloon a place that serves alcoholic drinks, similar to a bar

sheath a case or covering for a knife

snow hook a heavy piece of metal attached to the sled and which is staked into the snow to keep the team in place for a brief amount of time

snowshoes racquet-shaped items used for walking on deep snow

staked secured with a stake, a type of long pole or stick

summit the highest point of a hill or mountain

teetered moved unsteadily

towline the main rope that runs forward from the sled between the two columns of dogs and to which they are all connected; also known as a gang line

wicked dangerous and severe

1898 Gold is discovered in Nome, Alaska; construction on the White Pass and Yukon Railroad begins.

1900 The population of Alaska grows to more than 63,000.

1902 Gold is discovered in Fairbanks, Alaska.

1912 Alaska is established as a U.S. territory.

1959 Alaska becomes the 49th state in the United States.

Activities

Continuing the Story

(Writing Creatively)

Continue Ike FitzHugh's story. Elaborate on an event from his scrapbook or add your own entries to the beginning or end of his journal. You might write about Ike's Inuit family and how they came to live in the Yukon Territory or how Ike trained his dog Pika. You can also write your own short story of historical fiction about the relationship between Native Americans and non-natives living in the Yukon Territory in the late 1800s.

Celebrating Your Heritage

(Discovering Family History)

Research your own family history. Find out if you had relatives living in Canada or Alaska at the time of the Klondike Gold Rush. If your relatives did not live there, did they keep in touch with people who did? Were they Native American or non-native ancestry? Ask family members to write down what they know about the people and events of this era. Make copies of old photographs or drawings of keepsakes that you collect from this time period.

Documenting History

(Exploring Community History)

Find out how your city or town was affected by the Klondike Gold Rush. Visit your library, a historical society, a museum, or related Web sites for links to important people and events. What did newspapers report at the time? When, where, why, and how did your community respond? Who was involved? What was the outcome?

Preserving Memories

(Crafting)

Make a scrapbook about family life at the time of the Klondike Gold Rush. Imagine what life was like for your family or for Ike's family. Fill the pages with descriptions of special events, songs, family stories, interviews with relatives, letters, and drawings of family treasures. Add copies of historical records such as claims documents or totem poles. Decorate the pages and the cover with pictures of family heirlooms, hunting weapons, mining and dogsled equipment, handmade artwork, gold nuggets, and maps of the Klondike region.

To Find Out More

At the Library

Jones, Charlotte Foltz. *Yukon Gold: The Story of the Klondike Gold Rush.* New York: Holiday House, 1999.

Murphy, Claire Rudolf, and Jane G. Haigh. *Children of the Gold Rush.* Boulder, Colo.: Roberts Rinehart, 1999.

Murphy, Claire Rudolf, and Jane G. Haigh. *Gold Rush Dogs.* Portland, Ore.: Alaska Northwest Books, 2001.

Shephard, Donna Walsh. *The Klondike Gold Rush.* Danbury, Conn.: Franklin Watts, 1998.

On the Internet

Gold Fever
http://www.pbs.org/wgbh/amex/gold
To visit the PBS companion site to the gold rush documentary

Klondike Trail Society
http://www.klondiketrail.ca/
To learn more about the maps and trails used during the gold rush

On the Road

Anchorage Museum of History and Art
121 West 7th Avenue
Anchorage, AK 99501
907/343-4326
To learn more about Alaska history and see exhibits of Native American art

Klondike Gold Rush National Historical Park
Skagway, AK 99840
907/983-2921
To visit this historic gold rush area

Through the Mail

Alaska Natural History Association
750 West Second Avenue
Anchorage, AK 99501
907/274-8440
For more information about the gold rush and other Alaska history

About the Author

Pamela Dell has been making her living as a writer for about fifteen years. Though she has published both fiction and nonfiction for adults, in the last decade she has written mostly for kids. Her nonfiction work includes biographies, science, history, and nature topics. She has also published contemporary and historical fiction, as well as award-winning interactive multimedia. The twelve books in the Scrapbooks of America series have been some of her favorite writing projects.